Made in United States
Orlando, FL
08 September 2024

51301536R00017

ABOUT THE AUTHOR

Milo Scribblewood

Milo found his love of writing early in life. After some time away from his notebooks, pens, and pencils, he began writing fantastic children's tales to influence the next generation of young readers positively. He hopes to spark imagination and creativity in people and make this world a better place for all to live.

Milo lives with his family and Cocker Spaniel Carly in the heart of South Central Indiana.

The Adventure of
Tank the Turtle

Milo Scribblewood

This book is dedicated to all who came before me
so my project could come to fruition.

CONTENTS

LET THE ADVENTURE BEGIN

Tank the Turtle slowly woke up from his deep slumber at his home in Stump Stock Log. The beautiful sunshine slowly filled his room. Tank climbed out of the top of his log. He thoughtfully looked at his surroundings. The water was sparkly blue and crystal clear. The air above Stump Stock Log was crisp and refreshing. The sky was majestic; beautiful shades of red and purple lingered above as far as the eye could see. Snow-capped mountains could be seen in the background, far away. The way the sunshine penetrated the water created a magical prism of colors that always fascinated Tank.

"How does that happen?" Tank wondered.

He loved his home. Seeing all the beauty surrounding him filled his heart with joy. However, Tank loved adventure and playtime even more! Tank knew this would be an excellent day for an adventure! He was excited to meet with his friends and play new games, romp, and frolic at the Mighty Marin Coral Reef near his home.

The Mighty Marin provided safety and comfort for various sea creatures. The reef was made up of a system of beautifully colored coral. Every shape and size coral was a part of the reef. Every time Tank visited the Mighty Marin, he would see something he had never seen before. Sometimes, he saw new fish and other animals. Sometimes, he found new hiding spaces. Those hiding spaces would be handy when his friends wanted to play hide and seek. Once, Tank even saw a human far off beyond the reef! What Tank

wouldn't give to make it beyond the reef and explore the great beyond! He wanted to glide in the ocean and take in the strange surroundings! Tank filled his lungs with the fresh, clean air with a big belly breath. He slowly let the air out of his body. He smelled his Mama's superb cooking and decided to return to the inside of the log.

Tank's Mama prepared his breakfast.

At the breakfast table, she asked Tank, "What will you do today?"

Tank described his desire to play with his friends at the Mighty Marin. Mama became worried and chose to talk with little Tank about the importance of safety and not straying too far from home. There were dangerous currents outside the Mighty Marin that could easily take a little guy like Tank miles away from his home. Finding him would be nearly impossible as the currents constantly change around the reef. Some creatures exist out there that want to hurt Tank, too. She stressed to him that he should not leave the safety of the Mighty Marin Reef.

Since Tank had adventure and curiosity written on his heart, his Mama's advice and wisdom were lost on him. The opportunity for adventure and exploration charged Tank's soul with excitement, which was hard for him to contain. Tank quickly forgot about his Mama's advice.

As Tank left the log, he said goodbye to his Mama. She was worried that Tank's curiosity would get the best of him. Mama hoped Tank's friends could help keep an eye on the curious little Turtle.

The first friend he encountered on his way to the Mighty Marin was Dottie the Bottle Nose Dolphin. Dottie was sleek and slender. She loved to feast on shrimp. That was her favorite food!

Tank always marveled at how fast Dottie could swim. Dottie could do tricks, loved to play ball, and loved being with her pod in the open ocean. Dottie knew how to ride the currents created by the large human vessels and other large mammals. In the current, Dottie could relax and receive a free ride!

Dottie was a great friend to have. Dottie often passed the time by telling Tank stories about the open ocean. She would spin grand tales of danger, near misses, and the crazy escapes she made. Learning about what the sea had to offer was fun, but Tank did not quite understand the amount of risk associated with it. You have to be aware of your surroundings so trouble doesn't find you. Tank always thought Dottie was trying to scare him into thinking the open ocean was a threatening and dangerous place he should not go.

Tank's Mama attempted to do the same thing. Why was everyone so opposed to Tank having a fun time?

Sometimes, the Mighty Marin could get boring, and Tank felt he could handle whatever the ocean dealt him. His experience wouldn't be like everyone else. After all, he was Tank the Turtle! Getting hurt only happened to other creatures, never to him!

Dottie did her best to warn Tank of all the dangers, but she knew he was not listening. He was too busy daydreaming of what his adventure experience would look like. What would the water feel like? Was it colder than the water at his house? What if there were even more friends to discover? Were there more places and spaces to hide and play?

Once again, Dottie's sage advice went right over Tank's head. Tank was determined to find out for himself.

Soon after, they met up with Verna the Seahorse. Verna was the happiest and most grateful Seahorse in all the Mighty Marin.

"Hi, Tank," said Verna. "What are you going to do today?"

Tank replied, "I didn't have anything in particular in mind. Would you like to play a game?"

Tank knew Verna excelled at playing ball. Verna would get the ball, tuck it in her pouch, and go off into the depths of the sea. Once she got going, it was hard to catch her!

As they decided what to do, Bob the butterfly fish came and wanted to know what was happening. Bob was shy and wasn't in any big hurry to play games. He was a brightly colored fish with spots strategically placed on his body to look like eyes so his predators would get confused should they decide to go after him. Bob was primarily content to spend his days marveling at the colors of the reef and the seemingly never-ending inhabitants who called it home. Bob had a sharp eye. His eyes were so sharp, that his friends nicknamed him "eagle eyes." It's no wonder Bob loved to take in his surroundings. Bob, indeed, was a creature watcher! The others informed Bob they wanted to play ball, and Bob quickly volunteered his services to referee any game they wanted to play. They organized themselves so they could play a great game of catch. That couldn't be dangerous, or could it?

TANK AND HIS FRIENDS PLAY

As everyone took their places and with Bob looking on, the game started. It was so much fun to watch Verna catch passes with her pouch. Dottie could get the ball and do many tricks. Tank had a solid throwing arm. He could whizz the ball around with the best of them. This was great for Dottie and Verna, who loved catching long passes. Dottie passed the ball back to Tank, but the pass was too strong and sailed over Tank's head.

Dottie said, " I'm so sorry, Tank."

Tank replied, "It's OK. I'll fetch the ball for us."

Tank needed help locating the ball. As he looked down toward the ocean floor, he saw the ball! Tank finally found the ball! He quickly went down to get the ball so he could play fun games with his friends.

A glimmer of light caught Tank's eye as he was retrieving the ball.

"What was that?" Tank wondered.

He moved in to take a closer look.

TANK GETS HIS WISH

As Tank moved closer to the glimmer of light, his heart beat faster and faster. He could hardly believe what his eyes were seeing. The ball sat before a secret passage leading directly to the open ocean. The thrill and excitement of finally exploring the open ocean was too much for Tank to deal with. He simply could not resist. He decided to go despite his friend's and family's warnings. The secret tunnel was just large enough for Tank to scurry through. He was excited to go into the Great Unknown.

SOUND THE ALARM

Back at the Mighty Marin reef, Dottie, Verna, and Bob wondered what was taking so long for Tank to get the ball. At that moment, Bob saw a flash of light reflect off the back of Tank's shell. Bob knew that shell anywhere. It was Tank, and he was outside the reef! Bob knew his little buddy was in trouble.

Bob urgently called to Dottie and Verna, "Tank's gone out into the open ocean! He needs our help!"

Since she was the better swimmer and the faster of the two of them, Verna told Dottie that she should pursue Tank. Verna would go get Tank's Mama. Bob would stand watch in case Tank found his way back to the Mighty Marin. The rescue plan was activated. The friends had faith that it was not too late for poor Tank.

THE FRIENDS REACT, AND TANK'S CURIOSITY TAKES OVER

With a few powerful swipes of her tail, Dottie gained speed quickly. She could clear the reef barrier by jumping high out of the water. Her body, moving in a corkscrew motion through the air, gave her the momentum to fly further than she had ever flown. When Dottie re-entered the water, she was in the open ocean; however, there was no sign of Tank.

Dottie looked back at the reef and thought, "Oh, Tank, where have you gone?"

With tears in her eyes, Dottie frantically searched for her friend. The tiny Turtle was her best friend in the whole wide world. She just had to find Tank!

Meanwhile, Tank had already discovered an interesting rock formation. He was drawn to the rocks like a magnet is attracted to metal. He had never seen anything quite like this before in his life. Rocks could be fun to play on, and if they went high enough, there may be a spot where they poked out of the water that would be prime for basking in the sun. Tank had to know how high the rocks went. As he was exploring, Tank saw movement on the rocks. As he moved in for a closer look, he could start to make out several....... legs? What had that many legs? Tank certainly didn't know. The creature was also able to change color at will. Was this

some magical animal? Could Tank make nice with this unique creature and make a brand new friend?

"Hello," Tank called out with uncertainty in his voice.

"Why, hello", the creature replied. "I'm Imala, and I'm an octopus."

Octopus? Tank wanted to ask for clarification.

"An octopus?" Tank replied. This is the first time I've heard that name.

Imala explained, "We octopi have eight tentacles with suction cups. I can change color according to my surroundings so the bigger creatures can't see me. I can also move my body in certain ways, allowing me to fit into the tiniest spaces. If the bigger creatures see me, they can't get to me because I'm in such a tiny space."

"What is going on?" How come Mama never told me about any of this?" Tank thought.

Tank was just as confused as ever.

Tank asked, "Why do you live out here instead of at the Mighty Marin?"

"Ah yes, the Mighty Marin," Imala replied. "Many years ago, my ancestors were asked to leave the Mighty Marin."

"Well, why were you asked to leave?" Tank inquired.

Imala answered, "Many decades ago, my ancestors made lots of trouble for the other fish in the Mighty Marin. Since they had special abilities, my ancestors found all the best hiding places,

as they could fit just about anywhere. They got all the best food too. They would sneak into the cafeteria at will and eat whatever they wanted. The other animals that did not have our talents became very angry and bitter towards my kind. The other reef inhabitants wanted what we had, so finally, we were asked to leave and never return."

"That's terrible." Tank said. "You should be celebrated because of your differences and not have it used against you."

"I agree," said Imala. "But nothing can be done about it now!"

Imala inquired, "What are you doing out here?" You are too tiny of a turtle to be out here," said Imala.

"I have an explorer's soul and spirit," Tank proudly declared as he boldly stuck out his chest.

"Oh really?" Imala said. "If it's exploration you seek, you came to the right place! I know of a secret place where there is treasure. Shiny gold coins, jewels, and many other valuable items."

"You know where all that stuff is?" Tank said in an excited voice.

At this point, Tank was ready to jump out of his shell!

"Follow me." Imala slyly quipped.

With awe-inspiring adventures on his mind, Tank eagerly followed Imala into the deep, dark abyss.

Imala expertly weaved in and out of the marine plants. To Tank, it looked just like a magical forest. Tank was shaking with excitement. He was so blinded by his new adventure that he bravely swam on.

Twists and turns they took. The two finally arrived at the site after what seemed like a lifetime to poor Tank. They were both looking into the mouth of a giant cave! Tank had never seen such a monstrous cave in his life! He was in awe of the sheer size of the cave.

Tank thought, "If the opening is this big, how much bigger is it on the inside?"

"The treasure is in there?" Tank asked.

"Why, of course, it is. I have seen it myself," Imala said. "Step out in faith, my little friend, and your rewards shall be great!"

Summoning all his courage, Tank marched into the cave. He looked in all the cracks and crevices, but there was no sign of treasure. Tank ventured further into the cave, but still no sign of treasure. Irritated, Tank looked back at Imala but could no longer see her.

"The only way to go is forward," Tank thought.

So off he went deeper into the cave.

WORRY AND SADNESS FILL THE MIGHTY MARIN

At home, word quickly spread about Tank's possible demise. The other creatures shuttered at the bad news, filled with anxiety and sadness.

Verna had sped off to Stump Stock Log to inform Tank's Mama about her son's situation. Upon receiving the untimely news, Mama sat in her chair, a thousand-mile stare in her eyes. Verna could sense the sadness Mama was feeling.

"Don't worry, Mama, Verna said. We decided to send Dottie the Bottlenose Dolphin to look for Tank. Bob, the butterfly fish, is watching the perimeter of the reef for any signs of Tank."

This was of little comfort to Mama, as she knew the perils of the great beyond.

"My son, please make it home to me." Mama thought.

DOTTIE FRANTICALLY SEARCHES FOR TANK

Dottie had yet to learn where Tank could have gone. She swam this way and that, but no sign of Tank. Quickly losing hope, Dottie rested near a kelp bed. Gathering her thoughts and recognizing her sadness, her mind raced as she tried to devise a plan.

The ocean was enormous, and she had trouble figuring out what to do with no sign of Tank. Riddled with grief, Dottie cried out in pain. The prospect of losing her bestie was too much for her to think about now. She must remain strong for Tank's sake. She wailed again in frustration.

This time, Dottie heard a small voice. Was she hearing things?

"Why so sad?" the voice asked.

"Who's there?" asked Dottie.

"Look down here," the voice said.

As Dottie looked down, she asked, "Who are you?"

"I'm Coconut the Hermit Crab!"

"It's great to meet you and all, but I'm on a mission looking

for my lost friend." Said Dottie.

"Who's your lost friend?" asked Coconut.

"His name is Tank the Turtle." Dottie said.

Hmm. Coconut thought long and hard.

"I saw a turtle come this way not too long ago!" Said Coconut.

Dottie frantically asked, "Which way did he go?"

"You mean they, don't you? The Turtle was with an octopus." Said Coconut.

"That's strange, but there's no time to worry about that right now. We have to go! Use your claw and clip onto my dorsal fin so you can guide me." Dottie exclaimed.

The duo quickly sped off.

TANK IS....... GONE

Tank moved further into the cave. He still had not found any treasure. He thought of how disappointed Mama and his friends would be. Suddenly, being on an adventure seemed like a bad idea.

Just then, Tank felt the cave shake. It shook so hard that it threw him to the ground!

While on the ground, he heard Imala's voice cackle, "Ha-ha, you fool! You thought we were friends? You fell for my trick! This is no cave! Meet my friend, Gary, the Great White Shark! You walked right into his mouth and will soon feel the wrath of his rumbly tummy!"

Tank felt like a goner. His hope dwindled like a candle when it reached the end of its wick.

DOTTIE AND COCONUT TO THE RESCUE

When Dottie and Coconut arrived, they heard every word Imala the Octopus said. It angered Dottie.

"How could you do this to my friend?" she thought. Angry fire burned hot within Dottie. "Not today, octopus, not today." Dottie thought.

"That shark is humongous!" exclaimed Coconut.

Dottie spoke with a determined voice, "I've taken out bigger and worse than him! Hang on, Coconut, this will be a wild ride!"

Dottie sprung into decisive action. She swam toward the gills of the Great White Shark with an intensity never seen before in this part of the ocean. Dottie closed in on the enormous predator like a lightning bolt! And then…. KABLOOM! A direct hit for Dottie and Coconut! Gary, the Great White Shark, screamed out in pain. The collision was so strong that it tossed Coconut high above where Gary was waiting. The sharp strike sent Gary backward. It sent poor Coconut straight up in the ocean above. Tumbling toward the ocean floor, Coconut saw Gary's mouth wide open from the pain he was in. As Coconut plummeted toward the ocean floor, she saw she could clip onto Gary's nose with both claws. Coconut clamped down with her claws like she had never clamped down before. The pain sent shock waves down Gary's already incapacitated body. Gary's body rapidly descended into

the depths of the ocean. The undertow from his sinking body took with him a panicked and angry Imala.

Imala shrieked, "You haven't heard the last from us! We shall return!"

Then, out of sinking Gary's open mouth, Tank popped out! He was safe! It was the icing on the cake! Tank and Coconut hung onto Dottie's strong body so they would not fall victim to the undertow from Gary's sinking body.

The effects of the enormous collision were immediately realized. Dottie was dazed and lay motionless by an ocean ledge.

Tank pleaded with Dottie, "Please wake up! You're my best friend! Please don't go!"

Dottie's eyes slowly batted open. She was OK!

Tank exclaimed, "Oh, Dottie! I'm so glad you're OK! Thank you for coming to save me!"

Coconut slowly came over to the two friends. She had been tossed hard during the ordeal, but her shell absorbed most of the blow for her.

"Who's this?" asked Tank.

"That's Coconut the Hermit Crab!" Dottie chimed in. "Coconut actually led me to you! Without her help, you would have been shark bait for sure!"

Tank asked, "what do you say we return to the Mighty Marin now? Sound good?"

"Never better!" Dottie and Coconut exclaimed in unison.

The three friends laughed and grabbed a hold of Dottie's dorsal fin, and they slowly made their way back to the Mighty Marin.

LESSONS LEARNED, A GRAND REUNION, ALL IS WELL

On the way home, Dottie asked Tank, "What were you looking for anyway? Why did you want to leave the reef so bad?"

Tank explained, "I wanted an adventure filled with mystery, thrills, and treasure! I wanted to have a special story to tell you guys, so I would feel more like a part of the group."

Dottie replied, "Tank, real treasure cannot be found in the ocean or anywhere else. The real treasure is already dwelling inside you. Listening to your family and elders, knowing you have real friends who care about you. We all take the time to advise you and love you. We put the best of ourselves into you. That's the only treasure you'll ever need. Deep down, I think you know that. Hang on to those treasures for as long as you possibly can. Cherish and care for it; it will do the same for you. Leave the ways of the world behind."

Coconut added, "It's true, Tank. I lost my family at a very early age. They were swooped up in a fisherman's net. I never saw them again. Listen to what your loved ones say because you never know how long you will have them for."

As they approached the reef, Bob the butterfly fish was the first to see the trio.

Bob exclaimed, "They're here! They have returned!"

Verna and Mama quickly rushed to the reef's edge to meet our weary travelers.

"Oh, Tank!" Mama exclaimed. With tears flowing down her face, she whispered to Tank, "I didn't think I would ever see you again, my precious baby boy."

"I wasn't sure I would make it back, Mama," Tank slowly confessed.

Mama sternly asked Tank, "What lessons did you learn from this experience?"

Tank thoughtfully replied, "Listen to those who care about me, appreciate when other creatures invest time and wisdom into me, and always be aware of my surroundings."

"Good boy," said Mama. "Now, let's go home!"

CARING FOR ONE ANOTHER

As Tank and Mama headed toward Stump Stock Log, Mama suddenly turned around.

"Come on, everyone! Dinner at Turtle House tonight! I'll whip up something special for us to eat!"

"Hooray!" everyone exclaimed.

Homemade dinners always seemed to taste better when they were prepared with love. You could actually taste the love Mama put into her meals. Everyone savored the fantastic and well-earned food and laughed as they talked to each other. They truly enjoyed being together.

As dinner wrapped up and the gang returned to their families and homes, Coconut the Hermit Crab looked sad.

"What's wrong, Coconut?" Mama asked.

"I have no family and no place to go," said Coconut.

Mama could see the sadness Coconut had deep in her soul. Mama knew Coconut was hurting on the inside.

Coconut continued, "My family was taken by a fisherman with a net. I never saw them again. I've been surviving out in the ocean. It's a dark, scary place. A place I'm not looking forward to going back to."

"I understand", said Mama. "You may stay overnight with Tank and me here at Stump Stock Log. First thing in the morning, we will find you a place in the Mighty Marin Reef. There's always room for a heroine!"

Coconut was in disbelief. "No more darkness! No more worry! Yay!"

Mama proceeded to make a comfy bed for Coconut.

Tank went to his room and jumped into the familiarity and safety of his own bed. He slowly drifted off to sleep and dreamily traveled to a realm called Gold Mountain. Tiny turtles go to this wondrous place to re-energize their souls and rest their bodies, minds, and spirits.

Tank wondered what tomorrow would hold for him.

That is what makes life so interesting. Everyday is another opportunity to have a new adventure, meet new friends, and learn new skills and information. Take advantage of these rich opportunities, for you never know what path life will take you on.

Milo Scribblewood

ACKNOWLEDGEMENT

First, I would like to thank my Father in Heaven and His Son, Jesus Christ, who filled my soul with the words and inspiration to create this story.

Next, I want to give my wife a heartfelt thank you for encouraging me throughout the creative process and for giving me the resources to craft this tale. Thank you for always being there for me through good times and bad.

I send thanks and gratitude to my entire family. The lessons I learned from each of you led me to create this adventurous tale, and the lessons you passed on to me have been incredible and invaluable.

To anyone who has ever taught, educated, or otherwise helped me along my journey through life: thank you for the positive examples you set for me to follow. Thank you for putting the best of each of you into me.

And lastly, to the creators and pioneers of the internet, applications (apps), and other technology used in creating this story: simply stated, this book doesn't happen without you. Truly. I appreciate your steadfast devotion to your work and the daily honing of your crafts so someone like me could quickly reach the masses with this tale.